T0199036

Valiant Charlie Defeats the Sleep Monster

Tammy Lynn Laird

Illustrated by Daniel Majan

WestBow Press books may be ordered through booksellers or by contacting:

WestBow Press
A Division of Thomas Nelson & Zondervan
1663 Liberty Drive
Bloomington, IN 47403
www.westbowpress.com
1 (866) 928-1240

Illustrated by Daniel Majan.

ISBN: 978-1-9736-9294-2 (sc)
ISBN: 978-1-9736-9295-9 (e)

Library of Congress Control Number: 2020910132

Print information available on the last page.

WestBow Press rev. date: 6/12/2020

WESTBOW
PRESS®
A DIVISION OF THOMAS NELSON
& ZONDERVAN

Dedication

In loving memory of my father. He taught me a love for writing, harnessing the power of words to make a difference for good, and using those words to advocate for those whose voice has been silenced, ignored, or negated.

Acknowledgements

I would like to extend my deep appreciation to God who has guided each step of our son's dental and medical journey providing the correct path and the right people to help him defeat his sleep monster, to my husband who has held my hand and heart each leg of the journey, to our "Charlie" who endured much but came out stronger to help other boys and girls defeat their particular sleep monsters, and to the many family and friends who have prayed and encouraged us on our medical journey and with this writing project; we could not have done this without you. Thank you so much!

Foreword

It is an honor to be asked by the parents of one of my pediatric patients to write a forward regarding this book about their journey as a family, and on seeking answers to better breathing, sleep, and growth potential for their child. A mother's love and dedication to do whatever it takes to get her child better is amazing and inspiring.

I pray this book will help many other parents navigate the journey with their child who suffers from Sleep Disordered Breathing, or what we call airway issues that can hinder growth and development, causing potential long-term health problems.

As a dentist trained in identifying and treating patients with Sleep Disordered Breathing through oral appliance therapy, it is rewarding to know that I have helped another child grow to their full potential and be healthy. This cannot be accomplished alone but with a group of dedicated professionals who are focused on optimal breathing, sleep, and overall health for their patients.

Through the story of one child we can help many others navigate what can be a complex journey that can involve the need and help from other trained healthcare providers focused on airway health. Thus, it is professionally rewarding as a dentist in supporting the American Dental Association (ADA) policy that states the role of a dentist is to help children "develop an optimal physiologic airway and breathing pattern."

Dr. Sylvester Gonzales, DDS Round Rock, Texas

Foreword

"Valiant Charlie Defeats the Sleep Monster" is a creative journey through a family's experience involving the all too common problem of Sleep Disordered Breathing ("The Sleep Monster"). The effects of poor sleep can have a plethora of consequences. Great points the book makes are that with children, you need to catch them early and it takes a team of well-versed and experienced professionals; it is not a quick fix.

While I was the fighter pilot Ear Nose and Throat specialist (who specializes in Sleep Disordered Breathing), the book illustrates clearly that the results would be limited without the help of my dental/orthodontic, oral surgery, sleep medicine, and oral myology colleagues. We treat children and adults, and very commonly address multiple family members. I am blessed to be part of such a proactive and comprehensive team with years of experience working together.

I pray that families read this book and recognize that their family and friends are likely suffering needlessly from the "Sleep Monster", and will seek comprehensive help.

Oscar A. Tamez, M.D.
Board Certified Otolaryngologist
Head and Neck Surgeon

Table of Contents

School Used to Be Fun

"Don't be afraid Sam. You can be brave and defeat your Sleep Monster too."

"Was it scary for you Charlie?" asked Sam, eyes wide with questions.

"Yes, but Mommy and Daddy made sure I knew God would be with me and all would turn out fine. I even earned the nickname Valiant Charlie."

Sam held his beagle Beatrice even tighter. Beatrice listened intently. She was on her very first trip to an important place as Dino, her faithful friend had shared with her and the other stuffed animals before. This was a change in their usual school day. Though Beatrice was younger, she noticed school was not fun anymore. Her boy Sam would often lose energy when the mother read history, taught science, or gave math problems. Sam used to love math and science. Beatrice loved science most of all and told her friends she wanted to be a pediatrician or a rocket scientist. They were at this appointment to see about helping Sam breathe better and sleep smarter. Beatrice had heard stories from Buster, Charlie's stuffed animal, of the adventure he shared with his boy in their quest to defeat the Sleep Monster.

"Remember when school was fun? I used to love school until fourth grade. I tried not to make Mommy upset but it was too much to focus on what she was saying. It made me mad that I could not play but had to listen and sit still. I would get sleepy while reading and then Mommy would be mad that it took so long to complete my school work. I was just so tired and then hungry. It took 10 hours to complete the lessons. Daddy would be upset that we had all day to finish but didn't until after he came home from work."

Sam thought about the school days and felt sad that he made his Mommy worry about him as Charlie did before. But he was in second grade. Maybe that was why his parents recognized the same things for him as they saw in Charlie.

"I am in second grade Charlie," Sam stated. "I have two years before things get really bad."

Charlie smiled and replied, "I think Mommy and Daddy have wised up and want to take care of your symptoms sooner. Besides, you may not have to go through all I did."

The dentist, Dr. G, and Mommy explained to Sam with Charlie and Beatrice listening, that all would be okay. Sam had a mild condition and could use some help to breathe better at night. A functional appliance would be worn in his mouth to position his tongue and help him breathe through his nose rather than his mouth. His night terrors or nightmares would stop along with his night sweats and bedwetting. These symptoms would go away since now Sam would learn to breathe through his nose. Plus feeling more alert during the day was sure to follow. Charlie would continue to share more of his story with Sam as he recalled his journey to defeat the Sleep Monster.

"Why Are You So Small?"

Charlie was very quiet during dinner one night. His parents noticed his lack of constant yammering.

"Charlie, are you okay?" his father asked.

"Yes, just sad." Charlie replied looking down.

"Why?" his father inquired.

"Some kids asked me why I am so small. They did not believe I was a sixth grader. They said I should go play with the elementary kids."

"Oh. I understand son. It was like that for me too when I was your age. You will grow. Part of it is how you couldn't breathe properly to get that Rapid Eye Movement (REM) cycle sleep. Remember your Ears, Nose, and Throat (ENT) doctor? He said once you started breathing better and getting the correct sleep, your pituitary gland would release those growth hormones."

"Charlie," his mother began, "You have already begun to outgrow your pajamas…you are growing and much faster than you think. Do not compare yourself to the other kids…they have not been on the same journey as you."

His mother had tears in her eyes. It was difficult watching her son be left out and feel less than he was.

"God tells us we each have our own race to run. This is yours for now. Because of the things you have learned and experienced, good and bad, you can now help others that are just beginning their journey if like yours."

"You mean like Sam?" Charlie brightened.

"Yes son, like your brother."

Suddenly, Sam burst into tears. Everyone turned and looked at Sam.

"Sam? Did you bite your lip?" asked the oldest brother David.

"No. A kid said I am so small so others can do whatever they want to me, and it made me feel so little, unsafe, and alone."

The parents looked at each other and then hugged their youngest son. Another young boy would soon be on a quest to defeat his sleep monster.

Picnic at Night

"Lizzie, did you hear me? It is your turn." Flynn said as he waited for Lizzie to move in their checkers game.

"Sorry Flynn, I am just so tired. My child is very restless when he sleeps. And he chews or grinds his teeth which keeps me awake."

"Have you talked to Dino about it? He is the wisest of us stuffed animals. I thought the functional appliance was working."

"It was, Flynn, but something else is going on. I noticed how tired my boy is, along with the mother. She keeps me awake too since she hovers when my boy is sleeping. It is like she is looking for something in his mouth. People are strange. Personally, I am glad my mouth is sewn shut. She comes in every few hours too some nights. I will talk to Dino." Lizzie said while yawning.

Flynn beat Lizzie in their game and began cleaning up the board. Then, he said: "I need to go, the kids are almost done with school for the day, and that means they will want to play with us. I better go back to my room."

"Lizzie, Charlie may have a condition called bruxism. The functional appliance was working but due to the suspected bruxism, the dentist Dr. G is referring him to a sleep specialist neurologist so they can do a sleep study on him," Dino explained. Dino overhead the mother explaining to the father that Charlie had chewed through parts of his functional appliance and Dr. G suspected bruxism in trying to get air while sleeping. The sleep study would discover if and why he was chewing through his appliance. It was just a theory at this time and the study could answer other questions on sleep problems.

"Do you think Charlie will take me to help him?" Lizzie asked, wanting to help her boy.

"No, I think he will take Buster since he can withstand lots of tight hugging. Plus, his mouth is not sewn shut and he has a tongue. Dr. G told the mother of a tongue helper too," Dino shared.

"Oh wow!" Lizzie exclaimed, "If he did not have that functional appliance, our family would never have known he was suffering and struggling to breathe while sleeping! Could that damage his teeth?"

"Certainly possible. The mother made a worried face when Dr. G shared what can happen during those chewing sessions. I do not have teeth so just passing on what I have heard," Dino replied.

"Well picnics are fun but not at night when they can rob you of precious sleep and when there are no games to play, and no real food to chew," Lizzie stated while yawning again.

"My Brother Is A Cyborg!"

"Will it hurt?" Charlie asked Mr. Tim, the sleep study technician.

"No, but it will feel weird. I need you to drink this cup of water and it will help carry the noodle wire through your nose and down your throat."

Mr. Tim was filled with compassion but also quite assertive in achieving this necessary piece of the wiring.

Sam watched wide eyed and blurted out, "My brother looks like a cyborg!"

Mr. Tim smiled and stated, "I hear that a lot. Children are my best patients since they follow directions so well."

Charlie was fully wired up with electrodes that measured his muscle movements, breathing, brain waves, and the phases of sleep. His father stayed in the lobby and slept on the couch while Charlie was observed from a very comfortable bedroom. Computer equipment recorded over six hours of data. Only Charlie's father was able to stay, but they picked up breakfast on the drive home which was a special treat. It was a long drive since the sleep study location was in the downtown portion of the city.

The sleep study revealed some amazing facts. Because Charlie was not able to get enough air while sleeping, his brain would send him an alarm to say, "Hey buddy, wake up! You are not getting enough air!" The graphs showed that he was being awakened seven times per hour and it was clear, he had significant breathing obstructions. No wonder his sleep was not complete but rather fragmented. Because he could not relax enough, it was not possible for Charlie to reach the restorative phase of sleep where he would feel rested, nor the REM phase of sleep, when the growth hormone is released. The sleep study pointed to the need for surgery to remove the sleep obstructions.

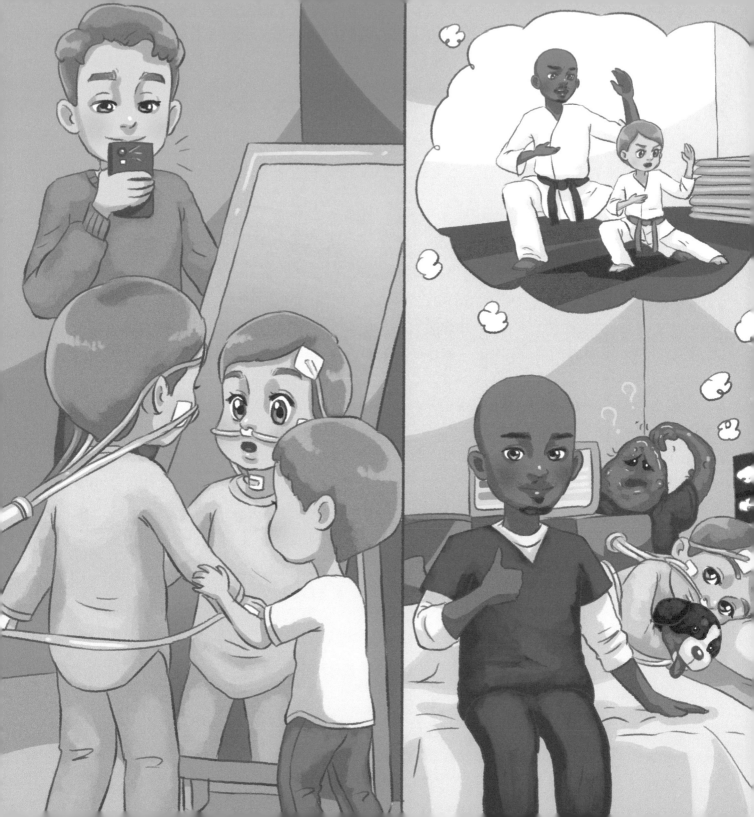

Charlie Trains for Battle

Charlie's eyes filled with tears. He and his mother were about to do more mouth therapy called Orofacial Myology to prepare for his upcoming surgery. He needed to strengthen his tongue before and after the removal of his mouth obstructions. He was scheduled to have his tonsils and adenoids removed, turbinates in his nose reduced, shave down his septum (the cartilage found in the nose that separates the nostrils), and have his tongue ties removed. The ENT doctor wanted this therapy done prior to surgery to ensure the best outcome. The therapy was quite time consuming and Charlie just wanted to be free. Was it not enough that he had spent over 4 hours doing school with his mother and brother? Now, 45 minutes to an hour of therapy.

"This is not helping Momma! I just want to be free. Can we just do half of what we have to?" Charlie's tears spilled onto his cheeks.

"No, we need to do all that is required," his mother replied.

True, there were times when she wanted to skip portions of the therapy too to avoid the sheer exhaustion and feeling like such a failure as a mother. But she reasoned that this was necessary and she would simply have to put her feelings aside, and do what was best for Charlie. In the back of her mind she knew doing the therapy with complete integrity would benefit other children down the road including little Sam. They would not allow themselves to cut any corners...period.

"Time for you to do your cave sucks and tongue to spot exercises," she said with a smile.

From the initial assessment, Charlie could not maneuver his tongue to make a taco roll. He had very little tongue strength. Now he was able to form a perfect taco roll and hold it for the 45 seconds followed by a rescue breath through his nose. By consistently doing the therapy, Charlie was earning his combat armor and being fitted with tools to defeat the Sleep Monster. Miss Willamina explained the goal was to replace bad breathing habits with good ones to develop the proper cranial facial growth for a properly spaced breathing airway. The therapy would lead to habituation and the end result would be to breathe correctly without thinking about it because of muscle memory.

"Very good son! This is our last week and look how strong you have become! Just a bit longer and we go back to see Miss Willamina so she can see how prepared you are."

"Can I play the computer after therapy?" Charlie asked seemingly strong after some encouragement.

"Sure, for a moment. But after snack, you need to wear your mouth piece," his mother replied.

The rest of tongue therapy continued with no more emotional breakdowns and Charlie was free to have a snack, wear his functional appliance, and go play on the family computer.

Surgery with a Side of Silly Juice

Charlie passed his orofacial myology tests with flying colors. Miss Willamina passed a helpful checklist to his parents; now they were ready to have their son go to the hospital as scheduled. Four seemingly ceaseless weeks had come to a close and the mother, father, Charlie, and his stuffed yellow lab Marianne waited for the sun to rise along with being taken back to the preparation room. The nurses smiled and moved with purpose in the pre and post-surgery stalls with moveable curtains. It was a center bustling with activity. People of all ages were either being prepared for their surgery or being cared for after their surgery. It was quite cold so the nurses gave out warmed blankets. After he had changed into their hospital pajamas, Charlie drank a tiny cup the nurses presented as "silly juice." Charlie's parents were quiet and nervous for their child but soon were laughing uncontrollably as they witnessed their son on that silly juice. Charlie giggled and made Marianne fly. Then he began doing his tongue therapy exercises. All that muscle memory had surfaced, and when the ENT doctor asked if Charlie had successfully completed the four weeks of Orofacial Myology, Charlie began to stick his tongue out and make taco rolls.

"Fighter Pilots are Cool"

Dino and Buster pretended to be airplanes while Beatrice watched. "What kind of plane are you Dino?" Buster asked as he pretended to fly very fast.

"I am a cargo plane and I can do many things." Dino replied.

"What does that mean?" Beatrice inquired watching her two friends moving around.

"It means my airplane is able to carry supplies and people. My plane has lots of flexibility. I can take off from any runway too," Dino explained.

"Cool Dino! What about you Buster?" Beatrice marveled.

"I am a super fighter jet. I can help people too by flying up high or down low. I protect people on the ground and target specific things," Buster shouted while running even faster.

Beatrice, the faithful observer of all the things the family did, pondered what her friends said and being one who took everything in at once, thought of Charlie.

"Charlie had to fly in both of these planes for his treatment. Not to mention the other planes he flew in occasionally on the journey."

Dino and Buster stopped moving and just stared at Beatrice. The others realized Beatrice wanted to share.

"How so? Charlie has been recovering and I do not remember the family taking any planes anywhere. In fact, I heard the mother tell the father that after the surgery, he was not to go anywhere until the ENT doctor said it was ok," Buster explained.

"Well, the Orofacial Myologist reminds me of a big cargo plane because therapy was necessary to help Charlie prepare for surgery. Just like your plane Dino, the therapist brought supplies or tools to help train and prepare him. And the fighter jet pilot in the form of the ENT surgeon, used precise movements to successfully pinpoint Charlie's sleep obstructions. He used maneuverability to go over the parts that needed to be removed and with pinpoint accuracy, he was able to make decisions quickly; he left the parts that were not bothering Charlie alone. The parents were so impressed that they called the doctor, the fighter pilot of ENT. He removed the obstacles flawlessly and now Charlie can defeat the Sleep Monster once and for all," Beatrice said excitedly.

"Which plane do you like best then, Beatrice?' Dino asked.

"Ummm, I like all planes. But I think fighter pilots are cool," Beatrice answered.

"I wonder what Charlie was doing during surgery." Buster remarked.

Defeating the Sleep Monster

As it turned out, the Sleep Monster was not as big a surprise as we thought. It had been within Charlie all along. Through the steps of his journey, he gained a new tool at each stop, be it knowledge or a weapon. Charlie stood covered in silver armor like a knight. He held a glimmering sword, carried a shield, and around his waist was his martial arts orange belt that armed him with information about the Sleep Monster. He glanced about and saw he would not be fighting alone. Standing by him was Mr. Tim, decked out in his full cyborg suit with a huge laser gun. Nearby, Therapist Willamina was in western gear and held a huge lasso; she also carried a saddle bag filled with useful tools. Dr. G stood with a huge sword and a box of assorted functional appliances. Above them was a special cloaked plane.

Charlie was taken aboard the plane after he met the anesthesiologist. Once Charlie put on his armor, the aircrew beamed the team down to fight the Sleep Monster. The plane could hover over the surface no matter what the terrain, become invisible, and direct other aircraft and personnel as needed.

After a short time, the Sleep Monster revealed itself and began to open his arms which looked like tentacles on an octopus. Therapist Willamina wrangled the tongue ties, sleep hygiene, and mouth breathing tentacles with her lasso and other tools in her equipment bag. Mr. Tim fired his oxygen enriched laser gun at the delta waves tentacle, and karate chopped the restless limbs and bruxism tentacles. Dr. G and Charlie swung their swords together to fight the V-Shaped mouth arch tentacle.

The aircrew commander, also called Air HQ, stayed in radio contact with Dr. G and heeded all of his recommendations.

"Commander, there is no more we can do here. The sleep obstructions tentacle must be taken out before we can proceed any further," Dr. G shouted while wielding his sword at the various tentacles with Charlie.

"Okay Dr. G, calling in the big guns," replied the commander.

The commander called in two fighter jets. The lead jet was flown by the ENT doctor. His wingman was the surgical team. Their mission was to fly in and take out the tonsils and adenoids first.

"Air HQ, targets have been successfully removed. Standing by for further instructions."

"Fly by the septum and nostril terrain to see what needs to be done," replied Air HQ.

"Roger that HQ. Identifying terrain...it is not as severe in septum so planning to use precision guided lasers to reduce inflamed turbinates," stated the ENT pilot.

"Proceed with caution…those radical delta waves may have some agents hiding in the turbinates."

"Negatory. Charlie and his allies must have gotten them. Moving to the tongue sector to remove obstructions and ties…those tongues will finally be free. They will need additional help in gaining strength. Probably need to call in some Orofacial Myology scientists to help establish their new 'breathing properly' system," replied the ENT pilot.

Air HQ personnel jotted notes on a clipboard.

"Final laser and review complete. Employing photo taker now," came the voice of the ENT pilot.

"Well done ENT leader 1. Head back to base and plan to inform the parents."

"Thank you Air HQ, we will see you all back at base. Over and Out," said the ENT pilot.

sleep hygiene
tongue ties
restless limbs
delta waves
mouth breathing
bruxism
V-shaped mouth arch

Recovery Ever After

"Okay Team, we are done here," Dr. G announced.

The Sleep Monster vanished as the jets flew by. The team was beamed back to the plane.

"Charlie, it is time for us to return to base too. The mission goes on for you though. Do what your parents say as they will help you get through the recovery. We want to give you these tools to remind you how very brave you are," shared the Air HQ commander.

"Group, Attention to Orders, we hereby present Charlie with this sword and shield to continue on his journey to defeat his sleep monster. Kneel."

Charlie knelt before the commander and then was knighted with the long sword. It glimmered as the commander touched his two shoulders.

"Arise Sir Charles, the Valiant. Please take this sword and also this shield. Now stand on the beam transporter. Farewell and Godspeed," said the commander with happy tears in her eyes.

The team all waved to Charlie and Charlie smiled back, thankful he was not alone during his fight. Around his neck, he wore the same medal as those on his team and in his hands, he carried his shield and sword along with his faithful stuffed yellow lab Marianne. He noticed his parents standing with the nurses, and how proud they were of him for being so brave.

Afterword

Funny how we get involved in things we know very little about, usually by necessity. I had no idea our family would be on a journey to discover why our son was struggling in school and inevitably other areas of his life. This book is to shed light on an obscure topic: Obstructive Sleep Apnea (OSA) and Sleep Disordered Breathing. I hope to hold up a lantern to help other parents and their children have an illuminated path to healing and proactive approaches, while the growth window remains open and viable.

I would be remiss if I did not thank the key personnel who helped guide our path: the two orthodontists who gave us proposed treatment options for our son's overcrowded teeth, the precious friend who shared how her daughter was helped when she used a functional appliance, and the third consult to a general dentist who specializes in more than just dentistry. It was this general dentist who treats all aged patients for health issues who would ultimately change our son's life for the better. A brilliant team player/ leader and force multiplier, he connected us with additional key personnel. He suspected bruxism which led to the sleep study and sleep neurologist, the ENT doctor, the allergist, the orofacial myologist, the inflammation/ functional medicine doctor, another sleep specialist medical doctor, and finally another orthodontist. This book captured most of the aforementioned stops along the way. Some stops became part of our fight while others were a one-time visit, arming us with additional information to fight smarter. All in all, it contributed to a puzzle and when every piece fit together, our son was able to gain the tools needed to fight his sleep monster.

Our journey still goes on as I complete this book. The surgical interventions and therapy, both orofacial and wearing a functional appliance, were able to reduce his sleep obstructions 50%. A second sleep study comparing his postsurgical state with his original sleep study, determined he was still contending with a moderate to severe sleep apnea or sleep disordered breathing issue/issues. After reconvening with the dentist, ENT doctor, and sleep study personnel, it was agreed that he needed more intervention. A third sleep study was conducted with titration to ascertain the calibrated setting for a continuous positive airway pressure (CPAP) machine. Thankfully, we are still in that viable growth window. We hope to sustain proper breathing while he sleeps to help him to reach all phases of sleep, including the restorative and REM, which seem to have eluded him for most of his life, as well as combat his OSA. During those 5 to 6 hours of titration study, our son woke up refreshed for the first time since he can recall. The hope is to help him outgrow his sleep apnea so he will not have issues as an adult. He has also returned to the care of an orthodontist to work on expanding his palate some more. With this possible expansion, he may be able to outgrow the CPAP sooner.

Our path is unfolding before us, but there is enough in this book to illuminate some ways for other parents and their children seeking solutions to begin their search for answers. The most important lesson learned is to keep pursuing solutions for dilemmas and answers for the questions you have yet to ask. Many of our questions were formulated along the way.

A particular observation that I feel is too important not to mention is how our ENT doctor conducted his appointments. Perhaps, this can help other doctors who may not already do this. After giving us his undivided attention, he took time dictating to a staff member what the findings were during the appointment and the disposition along with any follow up items. We each left the appointment with a documented sheet of what was discussed, determined, and any action items. This certainly kept all parties on the same sheet until the next appointment. I imagine it cut down on paperwork duties for the doctor at the end of each busy day. It also allowed the doctor to find closure with each of his patients for that appointment, and be able to move on to the next patient with their own unique issues. So, I am using this afterword to share this important practice. In the Air Force, we called it benchmarking. I learned the importance of sharing information and "benchmarking" to alleviate the pressure others were under, or gleaning from them when I needed help. Why recreate something when there is no need?

I also want to acknowledge the benefits of doctors and associated medical personnel who truly care for their patients. For these men and women, what they do to help others is a gift. Crucial items are not missed because they genuinely care. We have been so blessed to have such valued allies while on this journey. I wish it were this way for all, so patients are not neglected nor have incredibly important items missed. It can mean all the difference in a patient's life and the lives of their family.

Well, we wish you all the best and pray for your loved ones to defeat their sleep monsters too. God bless and Godspeed.

About the Author

Tammy Lynn Laird is a happily married wife, devoted mother, homeschool teacher, military brat, veteran, and writer. She is passionate about helping people and writes about the beauty found in everyday life along with the truths from the love of God.

Printed in the United States
By Bookmasters